Animal Antics

in words and pictures by

Janosch

Andersen Press · London

Translated by Anthea Bell

British Library Cataloguing in Publication Data

Janosch.
  Animal antics.
  Rn: Horst Eckert   I. Title
833′.914 [J]   PZ7
  ISBN 0-86264-033-4

First published in Great Britain in 1982 by
Andersen Press Ltd., 19-21 Conway Street, London W.1.
Published in Australia by
Hutchinson Group (Australia) Pty. Ltd., Richmond, Victoria 3121.
All rights reserved.
This translation © 1982 by Andersen Press Ltd.
Original edition © 1981 by Beltz Verlag, Weinheim, West Germany.
Original title: *Das Leben der Thiere*.
Printed in West Germany.

The Flying Frog

Once upon a time there was a frog who let all the other frogs living nearby know that he was going to fly. He said that on a certain day he would be at a certain place, and once he got there he would fly. Anyone interested could come along and watch.

"Fly?" asked the other frogs. "Fly how? With wings?"

"No," said the frog, and he told them that all of a sudden he had grasped the principle of flying. So now he could fly.

"Ho, ho, ho!" laughed the other frogs. "Yes, and break your neck! Wouldn't we just like to see you do it!"

For everyone knows the tale of the frog who once, and with great difficulty, climbed a tree, and thinking he was a bird fell straight off and broke his neck . . . .

Well, so all the frogs turned up at the right time and the right place. Some felt sorry for the silly little frog, others were looking forward to seeing him fall, but not one of them believed he could fly.

"He probably won't turn up at all," said one frog. "That's what usually happens."

But he did turn up.

He walked through the crowd, quite calm and perfectly relaxed.

He was wearing nothing but his old jacket, and a long scarf casually wound around his neck.

It did not look as if he had a secret little motor strapped on behind. But perhaps there were little wings on his paws, which he was digging into his pockets.

However, there were no wings on his paws when he took them out of his pockets so as to climb a little ladder, and then scramble up a plant. It would have looked like a flower stem to us, but to the little animals it was a tall tree.

The frog did not show off, like a circus performer about to attempt his death-defying leap, who might be expected to powder his paws or bow five times first.

Or at least to snap his fingers.

If anything, he looked rather shy about it. He simply took off his scarf and jacket and dropped them, no doubt to have more freedom of movement, and then he flew away.

They all saw him, but they didn't believe it.

If you keep a frog as a pet, you will sometimes see him sitting and thinking, wondering if he could grasp the principle of flying. And when he thinks it will be good flying weather, he will climb a little ladder.

No one knows if any of those frogs have ever been able to fly away. But we do know that when frogs climb their little ladders, the weather will improve.

Apart from that, we know nothing at all about it.

Valerian Hare

Down where the river winds its way across the meadows, flowing past the trees and bushes, the wind is blowing gently over the grass just as if nothing were wrong. Just as if the countryside were quiet and peaceful and full of the joys of life, with flies humming and honey-bees buzzing and bumble-bees bumbling about. God's in his Heaven, you might say, all's right with the world.

But all is not what it seems.

If you look hard and keenly at the blades of grass, you will see something moving.

Yes, there! Not as if it were just a mouse in search of food, either.

Or two beetles having a wrestling match.

Or a butterflies' wedding.

If that were it, the grass would be moving differently.

This is something *suspicious*. And you don't need particularly sharp eyes to see the wild dog's nose cautiously coming up out of the grass.

Or the snout of a bad little pig to the left, looking across at the dog.

Or a pair of rather battered rabbit-ears over to the right, making their way through the grass. No, it doesn't take any great brain to realize that *something is going on.*

Something not very nice.

For the wild dog's gang is out prowling the fields.

"Follow me, bold boys!" barks the dog.

His voice is a hoarse voice, sounding like whisky or brandy or rum. Like a pirate's voice after the pirate has been at sea for thirty-three years, breathing in the stormy winds and the salt of the raging waves. The voice of a thorough-going scoundrel.

Not so very long ago, this part of the country was a beautiful place.

The rabbits and the farmers worked in the fields. They sowed carrots and cabbages, sharing the work: some of them did the sowing and some harvested the crops. (It was the farmers who did the sowing.) Neighbouring creatures liked to come and visit, and all the little pigs and chickens and moles and jays would sit outside the rabbits' cottages with them.

It was like Paradise.

Then, one day, the wild dog came along. He went to the middle of the rabbit village and stood there, growling horribly. He bared his teeth, he seized two perfectly peaceful rabbits, tossed them in the air, kicked them through the dust, and that was the end of peace in the village.

"Anyone who has any objections, just step forward!" barked the wicked dog.

Nobody stepped forward. The rabbits hardly even dared to leave their cottages; they could never be sure they were safe, these days. The wild dog made himself at home, ate up anyone who got in his way, bared his teeth, and acted as if the world belonged to him.

So it did, too. Or anyway, Rabbitland did, down here by the river.

And since the rabbits did not want to starve to death, two or three of them soon came along – perhaps the most timid of the rabbits – and as

they did not want to be eaten either, they offered to serve the wicked dog.

"Okay, bold boys!" growled the wicked dog. "Follow me!"

So they went through the fields, and other creatures came to join them. They were a disreputable lot, with a good many shady characters among them, and some pigs, both large and small, and a rooster too, and an old hen. They ran wild, stealing anything that wasn't nailed down, and altogether they were a desperate band.

The wild dog called his gang together on a bare patch of ground in the middle of the meadow, surrounded by tall grass. There was a sinister gleam in his eyes. "Now, my bold boys, the terrors of Rabbitland . . . ."

"Hooray, hooray!"

"Today we are going to . . . ."

"Hooray, hooray!"

For the wild dog had said everyone must cheer him when he spoke, whatever he said. He would kick anyone who didn't cheer – hard, too.

"Today we are going to make someone king."

"Hooray, hoooooray!"

Did they think one of them was going to be made king? If the dog had meant he was going to be king himself, he'd have said so. Or growled so.

"Who? Who?" shouted the gang.

"Valerian."

At that their jaws dropped. Nobody shouted, "Hooray!" They all thought Valerian was the biggest fool in the whole wood.

Valerian was a simple-minded hare. He lived in a hut in the middle of a meadow, quite unprotected, without even a door or a gate. Anyone could have walked in to steal his things.

Steal his things – what things? He had nothing for anyone to steal, nothing whatever.

Valerian did not own anything. He lived on a few pawfuls of grass, or anything else he found, and he had no regular work and never seemed to do a job. Nobody knew where he came from or where he belonged. And wherever he went everything turned very peaceful, so that is why they called him Valerian, since the herb valerian is well-known for its soothing properties.

Valerian never lost his temper. If someone pulled his long ears for a joke he did not hit back; he was more likely to join in the laughter. When people needed someone to rock their babies to sleep, they sent for Valerian.

If somebody couldn't bring his hay harvest in alone, Valerian would lend a hand, and he usually ended up doing all the work by himself.

If a hare fell sick, they fetched Valerian. He would come and sit down, stay for a while and feed the sick hare until he felt better.

If people had no time to stir their carrots in the pot, they sent for Valerian. And Valerian never asked to be paid.

"What a fool he is!" they said.

They could even send for him at night, since he needed hardly any sleep. Even if he did happen to be asleep he would wake up at once and come. He would go to see anyone who was feeling sad because his wife had left him, or had been trapped by a poacher, and they would drink a little mouse brandy together until the sad person felt happier.

Valerian buried the dead, and played with the babies. He cared for mothers when the father of the family did not come home from hunting. He used to stay out in the rain, because he did not mind rain.

And when the weather was hot he did not get into the shade, because he did not mind heat either.

It was impossible to insult him – in fact, they all thought, he was a fool, a complete idiot.

"You mean you're going to make *him* king?" they all cried.

Even the hunter never shot at Valerian. Sometimes he would raise his gun, and then lower it again, nobody knew why. They supposed it was because the hunter thought he was too stupid to be shot.

Valerian Hare could walk through the humans' village in broad daylight, and no dog would chase him, no child would run after him. Why not? Because they thought he was so stupid!

"You mean you're going to make *him* king?" everyone cried.

"Does he have sharp teeth?"

"Or keen eagle eyes, or what?"

"Broken bones, that's what he'll soon have!" grinned the wild dog. "Follow me, bold boys! This is going to be fun!"

The wild dog's gang marched off through the fields, and went to the hare's hut.

The wild dog bowed low and mockingly to little Valerian Hare. "Hail, your majesty!" he said.

Valerian Hare did not even move.

They had not expected that. They had thought the stupid little hare would feel so proud he would jump for joy.

"Didn't you hear me, you silly little fool?"

Valerian Hare just turned slightly away, if anything.

Then they dragged him out of his hut and across the meadow to the level ground by the river.

"Don't waste time talking to him!" shouted the wild dog. "He's going to be made king, so there!"

They built him a throne which would look as tall to a little hare as the Eiffel Tower looks to the people of Paris, and which would topple over at the slightest breath of wind.

And they put Valerian Hare on top of the throne, so that he was bound to fall off and break his neck. That was going to be the big joke.

But the throne did not topple over.

Then the wild dog tied a rope to the bottom leg of the throne, and pulled.

And when the throne did collapse, something happened. Or rather, nothing happened.

They thought they saw Valerian Hare stay there, sitting in the air, and then float slowly down. At all events, there he was standing in the middle of them, unharmed. But they couldn't believe their eyes. They thought they must have been seeing things, and dared not say anything about it.

The wild dog frowned, and began thinking. "Oh, well," he growled, "he's our king now, so off to the village with him."

They surrounded him and went off to the rabbit village down by the river.

But nothing turned out the way the wild dog had expected.

The people of the rabbit village mocked their foolish king a little at first, but he had not been there for very long before a strange peaceful feeling came over the place. Those who had been living in terror of the wild dog lost some of their fear. They ventured out of their cottages

again, and fetched food from the fields. The wild dog lay a little way off, baring his teeth. Several of his gangsters had disappeared.

"We'll build you a comfortable hut here in the village," said the older rabbits. "A hut fit for a king."

But Valerian wouldn't have it. He said he didn't need anything. He already had all he needed, which was nothing.

They brought him delicious things to eat. "Sugared carrots with raisins!" they said. "A dish fit for a king."

But Valerian did not eat the food. He just ate a few pawfuls of grass, the same as usual, and that was all.

Two rabbits who were quarrelling about a bed of cabbages in Farmer Fred's garden came and said that now he was king, it was his business to decide how many cabbages belonged to each of them. But before they had even finished explaining, before Valerian himself had said a word, they stopped quarrelling of their own free will and went off together paw in paw. Now the cabbages belonged to both of them, and they left a few for Farmer Fred.

Soon the neighbours came visiting again. And the pigs, both large and small, who had been in the wild dog's gang, were friends with the rabbits now.

What about the wild dog? Well, the wild dog slunk around the village with his tail between his legs, growling and looking grim, like someone up to no good.

There was a savage stag in those parts at the time. He went about digging up the fields and ruining the rabbit villages with his antlers.

"Why don't you go and do something about it?" the animals said to the wild dog. "After all, you've been living here and acting as our leader!"

But the wild dog was afraid to go.

However, when the savage stag appeared in the village, his antlers waving above the cottages, they sent the wild dog out to meet him.

The wild dog slunk away behind a rock, but little Valerian Hare stood in the stag's path.

And when the stag charged, full tilt, Valerian moved slightly aside – only very slightly – and the savage stag swept past.

This happened four or five times, until the stag was worn out, though the hare was not, since he had hardly moved at all. The stag could not take proper aim with his antlers any more, and he rammed their tips so far into the earth that he couldn't get them out again. Now the people of Rabbitland need not fear the fierce creature any more.

When the wild dog saw that, he went away.

No one ever saw Valerian Hare move more than he had to. Generally, he looked as if he were doing nothing at all. He never bore a burden for himself. If people wanted someone to rock a baby to sleep, Valerian would do it, just as he used to.

When the hunter came by, perhaps intending to shoot some rabbits, he avoided the little rabbit village by the river. It was as if some mysterious power kept him away.

Soon everything was all right again, and none of the villagers quarrelled with each other. Nobody could say how Valerian had done it. Without using force, without sharp teeth to bite people.

Soon he went back to his hut in the lonely meadow, and went on living on three pawfuls of grass, and they forgot he had been their king, and took to thinking him a simple-minded fool again.

But as long as he lived there, everything was all right.

First Flight

"Your egg hatched seven weeks ago,
young chick," said Father Bird, "and so
it's time for you to learn to fly.
You'll soon be soaring in the sky!"

He gave instructions to his chick,
together with a hefty kick.
But sad to say,
the chick just fell . . . .

and so there is no more to tell.

The Good Child

"My child," said Mother Pig one day,
"be careful when you walk this way.
And don't go near that great big stone.
Mind you don't fall and break a bone."

The little pig was good as gold.
She always did as she was told.
She trotted safely round the farm,
and never came to any harm.

The Calf and the Cow

"I wish that I were grown up now!"
said Baby Calf to Mother Cow.
"Oh, growing up takes far too long!
If only I were big and strong,
I'd jump the fence and run away,
and in the meadows I would play."

"My dear," said kindly Mother Cow,
"I wish that I were little now!
For once you're grown up, big and strong,
the farmer there will come along –
and you'll be beef! Mark what I say:
enjoy your childhood while you may!"

"If that is true, I won't complain,
dear Mother, since you make it plain,
I should be happy with my lot!"
But those wise words, alas, were not
much good. Before the calf was grown,
the farmer took him off to town –
and he was veal, poor little calf!
Here you can read his epitaph:

Friends, you may learn from my sad plight
that Mother is not always right.

A Moral Tale

"I've warned you once, I've warned you twice,
my child! You must keep off the ice,"
said Mother Goat. "That ice is thin.
You might go through it and fall in."

The silly kid just went ahead,
not heeding what its mother said.
Pride goes, we know, before a fall ...
and in fell kid and scarf and all.

Tiger Piglet

One day the little pigs said to their father, "Father, we do so wish we had a brother! Will you give us a brother, please? Go on, do!"

"Well, all right," said Father Pig, and he went to market and bought them a brother. A little piglet– a pig brother.

But that was not what they had wanted. They wanted a tiger. *A tiger brother.* They had plenty of pigs at home already, being pigs themselves.

They moaned and groaned, and Father Pig said, "There weren't any tigers."

However, as they were moaning and groaning so much, Father Pig made them a tiger that night. He made the tiger out of their new brother the piglet, with paint and a paintbrush, working by candlelight.

How pleased the little pigs were! They hugged and kissed the little tiger, and started training him to be their brother. It was hard training, because they wanted a tiger brother– a brother who was not a pig. Who acted like a tiger and not like a pig. And the training was *all for his own good.*

First they taught him manners. He was such a fast learner that soon he even had better manners than his parents, for what that was worth.

Then they taught him to turn cartwheels, and be brave, and have a good head for heights, which is one of the very first things new brothers have to learn.

And they taught him how to go fishing without any bait or hook, something every great man must know if he is to get on in the world. They also taught him how to dive boldly into unknown depths, which is important in life too.

They taught him the dangerous but well-lit trick of jumping through a blazing hoop. Every good circus has a tiger who can do that.

When the time came for him to go to school, he knew so much that he amazed the teacher, and his brothers felt very proud.

They were the most popular pigs in town, and they all had a wonderful time!

Their tiger brother had a lot of luck with the girls, too, and some of that rubbed off on his brothers, as a small reward for all their trouble.

So after a while, they felt it was time their brother was crowned king. King of the Pigs.

"Long live the king! Long live the king, and long live the king's brothers too – hooray!" the people shouted.

Now that they were the king's brothers, the little pigs led a carefree life, respected by all and making merry: another small reward for all their trouble.

And so things might have gone on for ever and ever, except . . . except that one day little King Tiger went walking behind the fire engine. He felt like having a nice shower. He wanted to be sprinkled with the water and catch some of it in his mouth. And the little pigs' days of glory were over, because the water from the fire engine washed his tiger stripes away like rain. As he was not a tiger any more he was not king any more either, for the pigs did not want a pig for king, they wanted a tiger. They had plenty of pigs already, being pigs themselves.

So the little pigs gave their brother back to Father Pig. They said it was a tiger brother they had wanted, not a pig brother, and he should have *known* that.

Shouldn't he?

Father Hare's Good Advice

There was once a family of little hares, and when the time came for them to hop out into the world and earn their own living, wise old Father Hare called them all together.

"Children," he told them, "the time has come for me to send you out into the world to earn your own living. I'm poor, and all I can give you is a piece of good advice each. You just follow my advice, and you'll be all right."

He told his eldest son never to fear anybody or anything. "Courage is the secret of success, son!" he said. "Off you go!"

He told his second son that if ever he saw the fox he should go and get the hunter. For the fox eats hares, so he is their enemy, but the hunter – said Father Hare – kills foxes, so he is the foxes' enemy, and

34

therefore he must be a friend of hares and would protect Father Hare's second son from the fox. "It's quite simple really. Off you go, son, and remember what I say!"

He told his daughters to go and marry big strong hares who could bring home plenty of food. "It's a very good thing for a girl to have a big strong husband," he said. "So off you go, do as I say, and you'll lead a happy, quiet life."

But when he came to the smallest hare, who was called Gussie, Father Hare said, "Son, you're small and weak. You'd better beware of everything and avoid everybody, in case you get trodden on. That's the best advice I can give *you*!"

So the young hares left their father's house and went out into the world.

The first hare, who had been told not to fear anything, soon met the wolf.

He shook his fist at the wolf. "Want a punch on the nose, do you?" he shouted.

The wolf did not so much as twitch an ear. He simply ate the hare all up, and that was the end of *him*!

The second hare lay in wait for the fox, and when the fox came, he ran to the hunter's house to get the hunter.

"Hullo, a little hare!" said the hunter. "And so close to me I don't even need to shoot it."

So the poor little hare was dead and gone, and that was the end of *him*!

As for the girl hares, they looked for the biggest, strongest hares in all the wood as husbands, and they got them too. Their husbands could have brought home food by the hundredweight– if they'd wanted to. But they did not want to. They had no intention of working. They and their wives had twenty or thirty children apiece, and soon the girl hares' youth was gone.

And that was the end of their dream of a happy, quiet life.

But little Gussie took no notice at all of his father's advice.

Gussie did not do what his father told him: he did just the opposite. He was not afraid of anything, and lived as he pleased. He could follow the fox and the hunter without being spotted, because he was so small. He used to lie down right in front of people who were out for walks in the country. Sometimes he even let them pick him up and look at him, but he

would pretend to be dead, so that they wouldn't keep a very good eye on him, and next moment he was gone again, much to their bewilderment. Some of them thought they had been seeing things, and bought new spectacles which they didn't need at all. Some of them were never quite right in the head again, and kept telling their friends a lot of nonsense about the little hare they had seen, small enough to fit into a matchbox. One way and another, Gussie had a merry, adventurous life, and lived to a ripe old age.

So nothing turned out the way Father Hare had said.

Such things do happen.

Piggy Poems

Piggy Poem 1

This piggy grunts, in great distress,
"Who left my sty in such a mess?"
His mother does not care a fig—
"Why, it was *you*, you little pig!"

Piggy Poem 2

This little piggy needs a scrub,
and here you see her in the tub.
Once washed and brushed and nicely dressed,
the little piggy looks her best.

Piggy Poem 3

This little pig is filthy dirty!
But Father Pig does not get shirty.
He finds a pot of paint, and then
he paints the piggy pink again.

Timetable From 4 to 6

At four, Jack Lion sat down here
to toast his friend in ginger beer.

At five – so low the pair had sunk! –
they fell into the river, drunk.

At six, the fisherman came by...

and hung them on the line to dry.

The Piglets' Day

The piglets wake at seven and say,
"How shall we spend our time today?"

At eight o'clock it is the rule
for little pigs to go to school . . .

At breakfast (served at seven-fifteen)
they lick the plates and dishes clean.

...and light a fire, which soon burns hotter,
and warms each little piggy trotter.

The dinner bell is rung at noon.
Pigswill is on the table soon . . .

Then the piglets all go out
to kick their nice new ball about.

. . . and on the floor, and on the chair!
Tomato sauce flies everywhere.

They ask the hare to join the party,
and practise judo and karate.

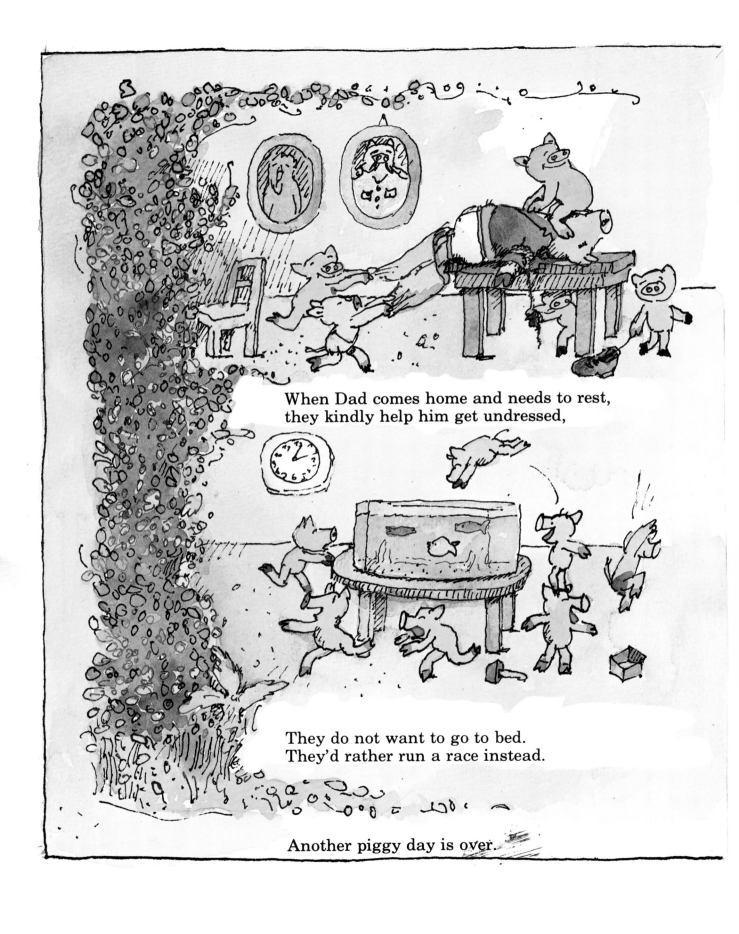

When Dad comes home and needs to rest,
they kindly help him get undressed,

They do not want to go to bed.
They'd rather run a race instead.

Another piggy day is over.

singing a cheerful piggy song.
They sing it loud, they sing it long!

Or use the fish tank (which is sturdy)
to make themselves a hurdy-gurdy.

Those little piglets are in clover!

Little Pig and Easter Hare

Little Pig and Easter Hare
hang their classy underwear
on the rowan tree to dry,
when the sun is in the sky.

Easter Hare and Little Pig,
having breakfast, eat a big,
fashionable Easter bonnet,
with lots of tasty flowers on it.

Little Pig and Easter Hare,
walking out to take the air,
water all the grass and flowers
with their special April showers.

The Wolf and the Fly

There was once a wolf who had a good dinner and then felt like taking a little nap, because he was tired.

Along came a cheeky fly.

The fly tickled the wolf.

Still asleep, the wolf hit out with his paw, but he missed the fly. The fly buzzed off, and as soon as the wolf was snoring again she came back to tickle him once more.

Half awake by now, the wolf hit out at her once again.

She buzzed off, but she came straight back, and this time she woke him up properly. She tickled him, buzzed off, flew back and tickled him yet again. The wolf jumped up and went in search of her.

She flew back and settled on his nose.

"You just wait, you wretched insect!" growled the wolf, though not very loud, so as not to scare her away. He wanted to take her by surprise when he hit her. So he struck out – cautiously at first, then with all his might. Wham! He did hit very hard, too, but he didn't hit the fly: he hit himself.

On the nose. It hurt badly, and made him furious.

By now, however, the fly was sitting on the curtains.

He went after her, hit out again, and pulled the curtains down.

"You want a fight?" he growled, but still softly, because he wanted to make out he was perfectly calm. "Okay, you can have one! But just let me point out that I'm ten times – no, a *thousand* times stronger than you are, you dirty little creature!"

"Right," said the fly, and this time she settled on his left leg and tickled it. "Carry on, hit me!" she said. "Ready . . . steady . . . go!"

So the wolf made his paw into a fist, for extra force behind the blow, took a great big swing, and hit as hard as ever he could.

He broke his leg, and the fly settled on the light bulb.

"You horrible little fly!" howled the wolf, less from pain than fury, for when you are in a towering rage you hardly feel pain. "You just come here and I'll tear all your wings off, and crush you, and . . . ."

But the fly was already sitting on his right leg. He tried to control himself, so as not to miss her again, and he hit out – about twice as hard as before.

He broke his other leg too.

The fly settled on his umbrella.

The wolf howled with rage, and she came and settled softly on his left arm. He took a swing at her and hit out in a blind fury.

He broke his left arm.

But she did not settle on his right arm, because he was going to need it to hit himself on the nose with all his might.

And so the wolf came to a miserable end. Battered to death by a tiny fly, because he lost his temper.

Tough luck.

The Mice and the Owl

Once upon a time some mice took an owl prisoner while he was asleep. They tied him up so that when he woke he would fall off his branch, and the fox would come and eat him.

Because owls eat mice, and foxes eat birds, so if foxes eat birds who eat mice, foxes must like mice . . . it was a bit confusing, but they had it all worked out.

The owl did fall off his branch when he woke, because he didn't have the use of his feet to push off with, and he lay there in the grass under the tree.

The mice dragged him into the middle of the meadow, so that it would be easier for the fox to find him, and they began to dance and sing. They sang and they shouted and they had a whale of a time.

Then along came the fox.

The mice never heard him. Either they were singing too loud, or there was some other noise in the air.

So the fox came creeping up – and who did he eat? First he ate the mice (he did like mice). He was probably thinking the mice might still get away, but the owl couldn't.

Then he ate the owl.

You never know for certain who your real friends are.

The Frog and the Mouse

There were once a frog and a mouse who were in love, and they wanted to be with each other for ever and ever.

"I know what!" said the frog one day. "Let's tie our front feet together. I'll tie one of my front feet to one of your front feet. Then we can do everything together, and we'll be with each other for ever and ever. I can tie a good strong sailor's knot that nothing will undo, and then we can never be parted all our lives! How about that? Isn't it a good idea?"

"It's a wonderful idea!" cried the mouse. Secretly, she had often been afraid the frog might jump away from her, or go into the pond and get eaten by a stork and never come back, or something like that. So the frog tied a triple sailor's knot that nothing would undo.

They found life was rather more difficult now, because the frog could not go into the pond and the mouse could not go down a hole. But they were so deeply in love that they put up with that gladly, and they were very happy together. For a while . . . because the mouse soon realized that she couldn't always see the frog's *other* foot, and someone in love wants to know absolutely everything the loved one is doing.

"Listen," said the mouse, "why don't we tie our other front feet together as well? We do love each other, don't we? Well, then we could do absolutely everything together, the way true lovers should!"

"That's very much the way I feel myself," said the frog, and they tied their other front feet together as well, with a knot that nothing would undo.

Now, however, they could not walk very easily. They often got out of step. Sometimes one of them went too fast and the other went too slowly, or else the other way around.

"If we tied our back feet together too," said the mouse, "they could do everything together as well, couldn't they?"

"Maybe we should try just one back foot, for a start," said the frog, for by now he was not quite sure they were doing the right thing. *He* liked to swim in the pond, but *she* liked to go down a hole in the ground. And now *he* couldn't swim, and *she* couldn't go down her hole. They were not really made for each other at all.

"No!" said the mouse. "Both back feet! You *do* love me, don't you?"

"Yes, of course," said the frog. And they tied both pairs of back legs together.

However, that was not a good idea, because now the frog could never swim at all, and the mouse could never go down a hole again. He couldn't catch flies, and she couldn't find roots. And so they led a miserable life until they died, which was quite soon.

"That's life!" said the big fat bear.

And he was right.

The Hare and the Mouse

An unusually small hare once married an unusually large mouse.

"That marriage will come to no good," people said. "One of them is unusually small, and the other is unusually large, so they're not right for each other. It won't work!"

But as it turned out, the hare and the mouse lived merrily with each other for a long, long time, and they were blissfully happy together to the end of their days.

Which just goes to show how wrong people can be.

The Wolf and the Little Pig

There were once two pigs who had an only piglet. They were afraid of losing their child, because they loved her dearly.

Kind Father Pig said to his wife, at least three times a day, "If only we could keep her safe from the big, bad wolf, the greatest enemy of all little pigs! What do *you* say?"

Mother Pig said the same.

So kind Father Pig told his child about the wolf. He talked and talked and talked to her about the wolf, and nothing else at all.

"For if you have just one idea in your head, and nothing else at all," he said to his wife, "you're sure to remember that one idea!"

Sounds logical to me. It was, too.

Since the little pig had never heard about anything else, she had just one idea in her head: the wolf.

She grew up, and she was nice and plump and pretty, and she thought of nothing but the wolf. She even began to dream of him. She was crazy about him.

Now the wolf happened to hear of this, because he lived quite close to the village, and as we all know, such things soon get around. Rumours can spread like wildfire.

And the wolf happened to come along one day, while Mother Pig and Father Pig were at market, and he knocked on the little pig's door. He hardly had to say a word, or make flowery speeches or anything, because the little pig flung herself on him like a dog welcoming its master home from five years in Africa, and she went straight off with him.

The wolf made the little pig very comfortable in his house. He fed her the very best pigswill. He brought her magazines with lots of pictures (she had never learnt to read). In fact, the wolf gave her a really lovely time.

But where would it all lead?

Well, before it could lead anywhere the wolf died, and was buried.

Now some said he had just been fattening up the little pig so as to make a better meal of her. But others said he sincerely loved her. Most likely we shall never know the truth of it, but at least the little pig had a wonderful time while she was young.

However, what is the moral of this tale?

Anybody know?

The moral of this tale is that you should believe what your father tells you, because in the long run it will lead to a happy ending, never mind how, and whatever you may think of it at first.

The Owl and the Donkey

An old donkey met an owl when they were out picking berries in the wood, and fell in love with her. He asked if they could walk along together, he carried her basket home, and then he asked her for another date. She said she supposed that would be all right.

They began to meet and have tea together quite often. Sometimes at her house, in the room with the balcony, sometimes at his house. They used to sit and talk.

One day the donkey asked, "Would you go on holiday with me? I'd pay, of course."

The owl said all right, but she would need a summer hat. "A Panama hat," she said. "They're the best sort." The donkey was so glad she would go on holiday with him that he bought her the hat. After all, this was the first time in his life he had ever been away with a lady.

"I'll come and pick you up tomorrow," he said.

When he came to pick her up the next day, she showed him her luggage. There were several suitcases, two or three bags, and a rug

which might come in useful for picnics. Also a hatbox and a sunshade. However, all this weighed rather a lot, even for a donkey, so they left all but the essential things behind.

"Oh, and I want to take my basket chair from the room with the balcony," said the owl. "It doesn't weigh much, so you can easily carry it. After all you *are* a donkey!"

And they set off, with the owl on top and the donkey down below. The donkey didn't mind carrying such a heavy load, far from it: he was delighted, because there is an old donkey proverb which says it is sweet to carry the one you love.

If the road went downhill, the owl would shout down to tell him not to bump her about, in case her hat fell off. If the road went uphill, she shouted to him to go faster, or they'd never get where they were going. As for the donkey, he never thought the way was too long or the road too steep, and the weather was never too wet or too hot for him. When they came to a river he would wade across, to keep the owl dry.

When they couldn't find a hotel where they could spend the night, he collected dry hay to make a soft, comfortable bed for his dear owl, and he warmed her with his nose.

When they came to the seaside they basked on the beach together, letting the sun shine down on his coat and her feathers.

They crossed the sea in a ship.

They travelled through distant, foreign lands, over plains and deserts where the sun beat fiercely down.

They once rode on a camel, to take some of the weight off the donkey's back – but who minds a little thing like a heavy load if the one he loves is part of it?

They journeyed far and wide, and by the time they got home again the old donkey was tired and thin – but blissfully happy.

And that, after all, is the only important thing.

The Teeny, Tiny Hare

A teeny, tiny hare was once attacked by a fox. The fox wanted to eat him.

"Don't you dare touch a hair of my head, or I'll beat you to a jelly!" shouted the teeny, tiny hare.

"Ho, ho, ha, ha, ha!" laughed the fox. "I'm not going to touch *a* hair of your head, I'm going to touch the lot!

And before I eat you I'm going to pull your ears *this* far apart! See?

Then I'll squash you into the ground with my thumb! Right here!

And then I'll swing you round and round in the air!

You midget! You little shrimp, you pipsqueak, you tiny little titch!

You pigmy, you!

You toy poodle, you teeny
little tiny little sugar mousie
hare . . . ."

Then the teeny, tiny hare hit
the fox so hard that the fox
saw stars . . .

. . . and the teeny, tiny hare
beat him to a jelly.
Who would ever have
thought it?

A fish went off on holiday.
Caught the wrong boat, went astray . . .

and soon the fish
will be served in a dish.

The Natural History of the Canary

told in words and pictures

The canary, also known as *Fringilla canaria*,
is not, as previously and wrongly thought,
descended from Man, but

the other way around.
Man is descended from the canary! This has
been *scientifically proved!* Here is a short
summary of the evidence:

I Canary in bath-tub   II Human male in bath-tub

Canary

The canary once lived in the tree-tops. So did Man. It was not until much later that they both came down to earth. Since then, they have lived happily together.

The canary will cheer old Granny up with his lovely song.

Man

He is equally popular as a cuddly pet for children, both girls and boys.

But as he is such an early riser, his morning song makes him a good deal less popular with grown-ups.

The canary does not usually have a job. He can always sing for his supper. On the other hand his wife, the female canary, does not sing, and is thus less popular unless she makes herself useful some other way, for instance, by doing the housework.

In return for all this, Man provides the canary with board and lodging.

Birdseed

The canary is an excellent athlete.
His long-high-jump and hurdles records
have gone unbroken since the turn of the
century!
On wheels, however, the canary
becomes . . .

. . . a roadhog.

So you will generally see the canary
behind bars, the proper place for a hooligan.
In fact, you hardly ever see him anywhere
else.

The Frog and the Goat

A frog and a goat fell in love and wanted to get married. The frog loved the goat for her sharp nose, and the goat loved the frog for his wide mouth.

People love others for what they don't have themselves.

So they went off to the cardinal bird, to ask him to marry them. The cardinal, who is red and comes from America, was the birds' and animals' clergyman at that time. He took marriage services, and gave blessings and said amen. If he felt like it.

"I ought to point out," said the cardinal, "that you two are not right for each other."

"Croak! What makes you think that?" croaked the wide-mouthed frog.

"Yes, what makes you think that?" bleated the goat through her sharp nose.

"Because one of you has a wide mouth and the other has a sharp nose, and they don't go together."

"That's just why I love the frog!" bleated the goat. "I love him for his wide mouth."

"And I love the goat for her lovely sharp nose," croaked the frog.

The cardinal knew it is no earthly use trying to talk sense to people in love, for birds are not stupid, so he said, "Oh, all right, then. Now you're married for life. Amen."

At first the married couple lived together very happily, because the frog was never at home. He was down in the pond, and if one of a married couple is not at home, they can't quarrel.

Besides, the goat liked eating grass, but the frog liked eating flies.

So neither of them ate anything the other one wanted, and there were no quarrels about their meals.

Then they had a baby.

The baby inherited its father's wide mouth. It could hop, and it could swim a little. It also inherited its mother's height, and her hairy coat. And it was green. You might have described it as a green goat, or a large frog that gave milk. A froat, or maybe a gog, whichever you fancy.

And then there was trouble. When the little froat was old enough to go to school, the school in the meadow sent it away to the school in the pond, because it could swim. But the school in the pond sent it back to the school in the meadow, because it gave milk. And going back and forth and to and fro the whole time is enough to send anyone round the bend!

Then a hunter came along and caught it, and as it is most unusual for an animal to have a green hairy coat, and unusual things are expensive, he made himself a green jacket out of it.

The frog and the goat did not stay married for long. They were *not* right for each other, because the frog had a wide mouth and the goat had a sharp nose, and these things never work out.

Precisely as the cardinal had told them.

The Frog and the Fly

A fly once fell in love with a frog.

"I love you so much!" said the fly. "I could eat you up!"

"Why?" asked the frog.

"So that I'd always be with you, and you couldn't do anything without me, and I couldn't do anything without you!"

"Why?" asked the frog.

"Well, that's true love. It means you could eat up the person you love!" said the fly.

The frog sat and thought. The fly loved him, and he loved her back. That was why he did *not* eat her up.

"Are you sure?" he asked.

"Of course I am!" said the fly. "That's how you know if it's a case of true love! Just ask all the other lovers!"

"Hm," said the frog. Then he ate the fly.

We don't know what the fly thought about it afterwards. All we do know is that ever since then, frogs have liked to eat flies.

Autumn winds are howling round.
Leaves come tumbling to the ground.
Rasputin the father bear
sweeps them up with loving care.

At last the job is done – and then
the leaves get blown away again.

Poor Rasputin – what a bore!
He'll have to sweep them up once more.

The wind comes back, and howling, "Whooo!"
Blows them away from that place too.

As for the moral of this rhyme –
sweeping leaves is a waste of time!

Rasputin, his friends are fearing,
may be getting hard of hearing.

This cure for deafness is a winner:
just call Rasputin in to dinner!

Rasputin the bear has made
a phone call to the fire brigade.

Asking them to bring their hoses,
and water his spinach and his roses.

The Farmer and the Animals

The farmer and the billygoat
enjoy themselves, as we may note,
sitting underneath the vine,
eating sausages, drinking wine.

The farmer and the billygoat
are freezing, even in a coat.

But once the winter turns to spring,
they will dance and they will sing.

The farmer is harnessed to the cart.
The ox will give the word to start

And two strong farmers in a team
will make the cart go like a dream.
Whether they walk or whether they run,
two pairs of legs are better than one.

The farmer gives us butter and cheese.
So feed him well on hay and peas.

Fatten him up on beer and rum,
and when he's fattened his time has come!
Take him to market and sell him; this
shows you how useful the farmer is.

When springtime comes you must drive all able-bodied farmers out of their stable.

But in autumn, when their work is done,
you must catch them all again, one by one.

We're waiting for the Easter hare
To bring our eggs around.

When he comes in, we'll jump on him
And knock him to the ground!

Ten Little Rocking-horses

Ten little rocking-horses
rocking in line.
One of them rocked away,
and then there were nine.

Nine little rocking-horses
rocking to the river.
One jumped into it,
but eight rocked over.

Eight little rocking-horses
prancing through the wood.
One pranced much too far,
but seven were good.

Seven little rocking-horses
sliding on the ice.
One didn't like it,
but six thought it nice.

Six little rocking-horses
sailing on the lake.
One horse sailed away,
and five had some cake.

Five little rocking-horses
going for a hike.
Four went all the way
(one was on strike).

Four little rocking-horses
climbing the fence.
One rocking-horse fell off,
but three had more sense.

Three little rocking-horses
swimming in the stream.
One of them swam away,
two began to scream.

Two little rocking-horses
wanted to get
in the water, one swam off,
the other got wet.

One little rocking-horse
looking rather sad.
If you don't want him,
give him to your dad.

Little Monkey

Little Monkey lives alone,
with a bright red telephone.
Call him, and you'll hear him squeaking:
"Monkey here! Who's that speaking?"

Monkey would like to hear from you –
And every word I say is true!

Little Monkey's house looks good
from the front – but if you should

glance at the bottom of this page,
you'll find it's just a monkey cage.

So do not trust your sense of sight –
And every word I say is right!

Little Monkey bought a bike,
thinking then he would be like

Superman, but when he dropped
off the bike its motor stopped.

So don't get in on Monkey's act –
And every word I say is fact!

The fox, I see, the fox, I see, does not much like the look of me. Trala lalala, trala lalala, trala lalalala lay!

The fox, I see, the fox, I see,

does not much like the look of me.

Trala lalala, trala lalala, trala lalalala lay!

The little hen, the little hen,
must get her legs unwound again.

Trala lalala ...

The rooster here, the rooster here,
could only find one sock to wear.

Trala lalala ...

The mongrel dog, the mongrel dog,
to kiss the rabbit is agog.

Trala lalala ...

The leopard cat, the leopard cat,
will kiss your hand and squash it flat.

Trala lalala . . .

The kangaroo, the kangaroo,
likes watching telly just like you.

Trala lalala . . .

The little pig, the little pig,
would like to dance a merry jig.

Trala lalala . . .

Here are four stories and eleven beautiful pictures all about Snoddle. Also featuring Snoddlemum and Snoddledad, Snoddle's sister Snoddlesusie (once), the Snoddlepony (once too), and Snoddle's friend the brave canary.

The Big-mouthed Frog

One day Snoddle heard someone croaking down by the pond. Croaking and croaking as if the whole world belonged to him. When Snoddle went to look he found a frog sitting on the stone, and it was the frog doing all that croaking.

"Why are you croaking as if the whole world belonged to you?" asked Snoddle.

"It does," croaked the frog.

"How do you work that out?" asked Snoddle.

"Because I'm the greatest!" croaked the frog.

"You're the greatest?" said Snoddle. "How do you work *that* out?"

"Well, I'm the most beautiful, for instance! Green is the loveliest colour in the world. Just try proving it isn't!"

That would have been a difficult thing to prove.

"So what else?" asked Snoddle.

"I'm the greatest at long jump!" croaked the frog. "*You* can't jump farther than me, for instance. Just try proving you can!"

That would have been a difficult thing to prove too, since Snoddle was no good at all at long jump.

"Well, what else?" said Snoddle.

"I'm the greatest at high jump," croaked the frog. "*You* can't jump higher than me, for instance. Just try proving you can!"

That would have been yet another difficult thing to prove, since Snoddle was no good at high jump either.

"What else?" said Snoddle.

"Breast-stroke," said the frog. "As it happens, I'm world breast-stroke champion. If you can swim better than me, just try proving it!"

And of course Snoddle couldn't prove that either.

"What else can you do?"

"I can dive, chase flies, sing soprano, sing alto, write poetry and

philosophy, ride a bicycle, paddle a canoe, smoke cigars, and . . . . ''

"And you have the biggest mouth in the whole world," said Snoddle.

"You're dead right," said the frog, puffing himself up.

"Positively the biggest mouth ever!" said Snoddle.

"I keep telling you, don't I?" croaked the frog. "I'm the greatest at everything!"

"Your mouth is certainly greater than all the rest of you!" said Snoddle.

"You're not so stupid as you look," said the frog. "Not when it comes to grasping facts!"

"Of course, if you want me to believe you," said Snoddle, "you'll have to open that big mouth until it's so big I can't see you any more!"

"Nothing easier!" croaked the frog. "I'm the greatest, and so is my mouth!"

And he opened his mouth so wide that it was bigger than himself – and he swallowed himself up.

So that was the end of him.

"That's what comes of conceit," said Snoddle.

And Snoddle was right.

The Tandem with Front-wheel Drive

Once Snoddle had a tandem. A red one!

A tandem is a bicycle with room for two people. One sits in front and the other sits behind, and they both push the pedals.

The good thing about a tandem is that you can take a friend for a ride with you. The bad thing about a tandem is that you need a friend with long legs to reach down to the pedals, and strong leg muscles for pedalling. Your friend must also *want* to ride a tandem!

Well, Snoddle had several friends.

His best friend was the canary, but the canary would be no use. He was good at flying, not cycling. He had strong wings, not strong legs. And he certainly wouldn't *want* to ride a tandem, because flying is faster.

Snoddle's other good friend was the Snoddlepony.

The Snoddlepony would be no use, because her legs were too short to reach far enough down; in fact she wouldn't even have been able to touch the pedals. And she would not have wanted to ride a tandem either, because horses are good at galloping, not cycling.

Then there was Snoddle's sister, Snoddlesusie. She was no good: you don't go riding tandems with your sister. Sisters are too cheeky. Sisters are too pig-headed. Sisters want to turn left when they're supposed to turn right, and the other way around.

So Snoddle never rode his tandem, which was a pity.

But Snoddle was no fool.

Rudolph Hare lived down by the willow trees. Rudolph was a bit of a fool – mad as a March hare, some said: didn't care about anything and didn't want to know.

But the muscles in his legs were like iron.

Now Rudolph was very pig-headed. Rudolph did everything wrong. If you asked him to do something, he did just the opposite, to be awkward. It was important to know that.

Snoddle pushed his tandem down to the willow trees.

"What's that?" asked Rudolph.

"None of your business," said Snoddle.

"Go on, tell us!"

"No."

"Is it a bike?" asked Rudolph.

"Better than a bike," said Snoddle.

"Is it a motor-bike?"

"Better than a motor-bike."

"What is it, then? Do tell me!" Rudolph sniffed the tyres and the saddles and the spokes. "Come on, tell me!"

"It's *two* bikes," said Snoddle.

"Has it got an engine, then?"

"Well, it soon *will* have an engine. Sort of," said Snoddle. That part of it was still a secret, but you'll soon find out what he meant.

"Let me have a go on it!" said Rudolph.

"No," said Snoddle.

"Why not?"

"Because it's a bicycle made for *two*. The stronger person sits in front and the weaker person sits behind. The clever one goes in front and the stupid one goes behind."

"Then I must sit in front," said Rudolph, "and you must sit behind!"

"No, the other way around!" said Snoddle. "Me in front, you behind."

They went on arguing like this for quite a while, and as Rudolph was so keen to get his own way, he naturally ended up sitting in front.

And Snoddle sat behind.

Now another good thing about a tandem is that the rider in front can't see what the rider behind is doing. So the rider behind can do as he likes: for instance, he needn't pedal at all. He can just sit there and watch the world go by.

Which was exactly what Snoddle did. He just sat there, and Rudolph sat in front, pedalling away like a racing cyclist.

"Sure you're not feeling weak?" called Snoddle. "Because if you are, you ought to change places and sit behind."

"Of course I'm not feeling weak," shouted stupid Rudolph Hare. And he pedalled away, carrying Snoddle along at a great pace.

"I'll sit in front tomorrow," said Snoddle, when they got home that evening. "I may be stronger than you after all!"

"Oh no, you're not," said Rudolph. "Anyone can see I'm stronger!"

And so he pedalled Snoddle round the country all day and every day, and they had a lovely time.

At least, Snoddle had a lovely time, and he saw all sorts of things.

Bottle Post

Snoddledad is called Snoddledad because he is the father of the family. Snoddlemum is called Snoddlemum – well, you can see why. Snoddlesusie is Snoddle's sister. She's as cheeky as a midge in May. Snoddlepony likes to eat honeyflowers because she loves them so much. That's the way it is.

Snoddledad goes to work every morning because he is the father of the family. He goes down to the river with his long pole and sits on a tree trunk. "My job is watching the river to make sure nobody drowns," says Snoddledad. "I have to save their lives."

Snoddledad has already saved the lives of eleven butterflies and two maybugs, and he would have saved the life of a baby fish too, only the fish happened to have learnt to swim.

Sometimes Snoddledad fishes other interesting things out of the river too. Flotsam and jetsam, little bits of treasure trove.

And today a letter comes floating downstream by bottle post. If you are sending a message by bottle post you must put it in a bottle and cork the bottle up so that it floats and doesn't sink. The message itself may be a secret too. It could be a map drawn by a pirate whose ship sank, and he came ashore on a desert island, all alone. But he knew where there was buried treasure, and as he would soon be dead he wanted to tell someone else where to find the treasure, because it would be a pity if nobody ever dug it up.

Or say somebody wants to send the world some good news: he can write it on a piece of paper, put it in a bottle, cork up the bottle, and throw it in the sea!

That is how the bottle post works.

Watch out, Snoddledad, catch that bottle! Well fished! He's got it under his arm. Snoddle will be pleased.

"Oh, a bottle!" cries Snoddle.

"No, it's a letter that came by bottle post," says Snoddledad. "There's a piece of paper in the bottle."

So let's hope Snoddle can read.

Of course he can!

"What does it say, Snoddle?" askes Snoddledad.

The letter in the bottle says:

Whoever reads this need never be afraid again

What good news! It's worth much more than money or treasure. Anyone would be pleased to get news like that! Snoddle should sleep well tonight.

Goodnight, Snoddle.

"Goodnight," says Snoddle. "See you tomorrow!"

119

Alone up in the Air

Some days go wrong right from the start.

You wake up early and get out of bed the wrong side, and you know straight away that today is going to be no earthly use, it will be a terrible day, and you might as well give up on it at once.

Today was one of those days.

Snoddle got out of bed the wrong side and immediately trod on his hat. That was a very bad sign, for we all know the proverb: "When the Snoddle steps on his hat, the day will be gloomy and black as a bat. But when the Snoddle steps on the ladder, the day will soon get gladder and gladder."

Snoddle kicked his hat up in the air, and it got caught on the light bulb. He couldn't find one shoe, and altogether the day was a failure before it had even begun.

No sooner had Snoddle made his first brave plans for trying to retrieve what he could of it than kind Snoddlemum called, "Go and fetch some water from the river, son! And mind you don't fall in."

Snoddle went to look for the bucket, couldn't find it, and had a long search. He filled it with water from the river, and sloshed some over his shoes. And carrying the water uphill, he fell into the bucket.

As was only to be expected.

Then they told him to comb the grass outside the door, to tidy it up for Sunday.

Then they told him to plait his sister Snoddlesusie's pigtail.

Then they told him to chase the woodworms out of the wood.

Then they told him to weed the wild strawberry bed, and feed the ants, and pick honeyflowers for the Snoddlepony, and do this and that and the other, and it was enough to drive anybody round the bend.

So Snoddle threw his hat on the floor and left his father and mother

and sister, his home and his own bed, for ever and ever. He was going off into the unknown, and no one would find him again as long as he lived!

"Hey, Snoddle, you forgot your hat!" I shouted after him. "And there won't be anyone to look after you where you're going!"

"I don't *want* anyone to look after me," said Snoddle.

"And what about the letter you got by bottle post, saying whoever read it need never be afraid of anything again?"

"Don't need it, don't want it, and that's all I'm saying!" shouted Snoddle, and off he went into the unknown.

He took a rope ladder and a bit of string with him.

He came to a meadow and went up to the tallest plant in it. It was tall as a tree. He tied the rope ladder to the piece of string.

He threw the string over the first branch.

Then he hauled the rope ladder into place and climbed it. From the first branch he threw it up to the next branch, hauled it into place, and climbed it – and so he went on, up and up, until the world underneath looked tiny, like a flea circus.

He threw the ladder and the string down to the ground, so that nobody could reach him.

He was never going to climb down again. Never! He was going to starve to death up here, where nobody would find him. And they could all fetch their own water, and plait their own pigtails, and comb the grass and feed the ants and do all those other boring jobs for themselves! They'd miss him, and then they'd be sorry.

It was nice up there. The sun was shining, and he could hear a cricket chirping far away.

But then the plant – or perhaps I should say the tree – began to shake.

"I hope it stops soon!" said Snoddle. His head was beginning to go round.

However, it did not stop.

Well, never mind, thought Snoddle. I'll be dead all the sooner, and the wind will carry me away.

Hawks circled alone in the sky.

Then there was a great silence. Snoddle could not hear the bees humming any more, or the birds singing, and he was hungry. It got very hot as the sun went south: the heat of noon.

Then it became even quieter, and even lonelier: the silence of evening.

And then it grew cold as the sun turned westward and sank: the chill and the terrors of night.

Snoddle could not sleep for terror. His terror was bigger than the world, higher than the sky, and it went on and on. Snoddle was trembling like an aspen leaf, and that night seemed as long as an elephant's whole life.

Then the sun rose, but things did not improve.

And when there was no way out for Snoddle, and everything was over, or *almost* over – someone came flying through the air.

It was the canary. He had been looking for Snoddle all day yesterday, and ever since sunrise today, and at last he had found him. "Hey, Snoddle!" called the canary. "Hang on to my wing!"

And down they flew.

When they got to the bottom of the plant, Snoddle was weak as water, but the Snoddlepony was there, and she let him ride her, just for once. She carried him home, and when he got home Snoddlemum baked him a cake with raisins in it.

I can tell you, it's a very good thing to have a friend who can fly. And another friend who is a pony and will always let you ride her, just for once. And a Snoddlemum who can bake you a cake. And has raisins to put in it.

Life is good, after all.

In the end.

Contents